when CHRISTMAS feels like HOME

by GRETCHEN GRIFFITH

illustrated by CAROLINA FARIAS

ALBERT WHITMAN & COMPANY

CHICAGO, ILLINOIS

To children who move
—G.G.

Dedicated to Daniel Goldin and Mela Bolinao
—C.F.

Library of Congress Cataloging-in-Publication data is on file with the publisher.

Text copyright © 2013 by Gretchen Griffith
Illustrations copyright © 2013 by Carolina Farias
Published in 2013 by Albert Whitman & Company
ISBN 978-0-8075-8872-7
Printed in China.
10 9 8 7 6 5 4 3 2 1 NP 18 17 16 15 14 13

The design is by Stephanie Bart-Horvath.

For more information about Albert Whitman & Company,
visit our web site at www.albertwhitman.com.

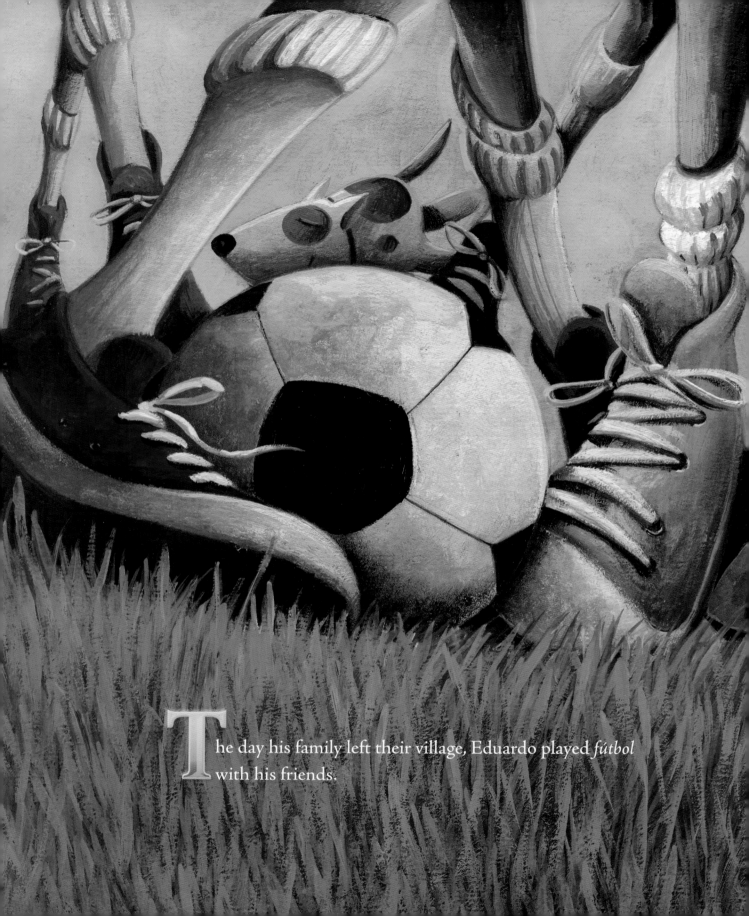

The day his family left their village, Eduardo played *fútbol* with his friends.

When his father said, "We must go. *¡Vamos!*" Eduardo picked up the ball and climbed into his uncle's van with his family.

His friends all went home, but Eduardo couldn't. His home was not in this village now. It was far away on a street named Sleepy Tree Lane.

Eduardo made sure his family's Christmas box was with him. Inside was the Nativity, *El Nacimiento*, he had made with his grandfather. Last year *Abuelo* helped him carve the manger from a piece of wood they found in the canal. This Christmas, though, it would decorate a different home.

He held the box on his lap as they drove from the village. His head rested on it like a pillow as they sped past rows of silky corn in the fields and inched under bright streetlights in the cities.

His feet tapped a rhythm on the side of the box as they crossed the hills and the valleys and the muddy rivers.

When the long trip was over, he carried the box into their new house and put it in a special corner. He ran outside when he heard a school bus clunk to a stop. A noisy group of boys jumped off. They shouted. They ran. Just like his friends at home.

Eduardo understood one word, "football." But the ball the boys played with was long and shaped like a giant egg. It dropped and bounced in zigzags.

"Football," a boy said again. "Want to play?" he asked Eduardo.

Eduardo rushed to the van and found his *fútbol*.
He held it up for them to see. *"Fútbol,"* he said.
He dribbled it around everyone.

They played football
and they played *fútbol*.
Then they all went home.

But Eduardo didn't want to go to this house. "I want to go home," he said.

"Sleepy Tree Lane is our home now," said Papi. "Tío Miguel and Tía Sofia learned to make this their home. We will too."

Mami put her arm around Eduardo. "It will feel like home soon enough," she said.
"When?" Eduardo asked. "*¿Cuándo?*"
"When we open the Christmas box," she said.
"Now?" asked Eduardo. "*¿Ahora?*"

"No, some things take time," Tío Miguel said. He pointed to the mountain that they could see from their new house. "First that mountain will turn the color of the sun."

Eduardo looked at the mountain. "That can't happen," he said. "*No se puede.*"

"But it will."

Then Tío Miguel pointed to a field. "And those pumpkins will smile."

"That can't happen. *No se puede.*"

"And the trees will become like standing skeletons."

"That can't happen, Tío Miguel," Eduardo said.

"Watch and you will see."

Eduardo started school the next morning, but this school did not look like his other school. "Have a great day," Tía Sofía whispered in his ear. "*Que tengas un buen día*."

"When will this feel like my school?" Eduardo whispered back.

"When your words float like clouds from your mouth," Tía Sofía said.

"That can't happen," Eduardo said. "*No se puede*."

When he spoke to his new teacher, Eduardo didn't see words floating from his mouth, but he did see his football friends waiting by the door. When he spoke to them in Spanish, they shook their heads, "No." When they spoke to him in English, he shook his head, "No."

When the class read a poem, they pointed to the words. But when the teacher assigned a math problem, he didn't need help. He knew exactly what to do.

"Mami!" he shouted. "It's time to open the Christmas box."

Mami smiled. "Yes. Now, *ahora*."

He pulled the box from the corner where it had been waiting and he dumped its contents on the floor.

He helped his mother arrange the Nativity, *El Nacimiento*. In the center of it all, Eduardo placed the manger he and *Abuelo* had carved.

In the early hours of Christmas Day, Eduardo filled the empty manger with *El Niño*, the Christ child. He looked at his family gathered around him.

"Now. *Ahora*," he said. "This is home."

After school he jumped off the bus with the boys. They all shouted. They all ran. Just like his friends in the village. They played football and they played *fútbol* and then they all went home.

But it still wasn't home to Eduardo.

Eduardo rode the bus to school every day. His foot tapped a rhythm on the seat in front of him as the bus inched around the curvy hills. He used his book bag for a pillow as the bus sped past the green mountainsides.

Each day he saw more blotches of red on the tips of the trees. He saw patches of yellow and orange. The mountain was turning the color of the sun.

One Saturday morning Tía Sofia said, "Today we'll pick your pumpkin. It must be round and fat but not too heavy."

Eduardo stepped over small pumpkins. He leaped over gigantic ones. At last he found the perfect pumpkin.

Tío Miguel drew a face on it and cut a hole in the top. Eduardo scooped out the slimy seeds. Papi carved the pumpkin. It was smiling. So was Eduardo.

That night the wind howled and swirled and tugged at the leaves. When he walked outside the next morning, Eduardo felt cold. The trees looked like bony-fingered skeletons. His breath puffed like clouds from his mouth.

"I saw my words float away," he told Tía Sofia. "But it doesn't feel like home yet. The Christmas box is still in the corner."

"Oh, but there is one more sign," Tío Miguel said. "Trees will ride on cars."

"*No se puede.* That can't happen, even here." Then Eduardo thought about mountains that turn the color of the sun, pumpkins that smile, trees that look like skeletons, and words that float in the air.

"Maybe it can," he said.

Eduardo worked hard at school. His friends taught him English words. He taught them Spanish words. They helped him with reading. He helped them with math. He learned to catch a football. He showed them how to dribble a *fútbol*.

He ate Thanksgiving turkey with them. They ate *tortillas* with him.
And for the first time, Eduardo forgot to ask about the Christmas box.

One afternoon, he saw cars coming from the tree farm where Papi worked. They had long green bundles on top.

His friend pointed at the cars. "Look! It's almost Christmas," he said.

"That's it!" Eduardo said. "Trees are riding on cars." He rushed down Sleepy Tree Lane to his home.